How Do Dinosaurs Play with Their Friends?

SCHOLASTIC INC.
New York Toronto London Auckland Sydney
Mexico City New Delhi Hong Kong Buenos Aires

These books were originally published in hardcover by the Blue Sky Press in 2006.

ISBN-13: 978-0-545-01979-8
ISBN-10: 0-545-01979-6

How Do Dinosaurs Learn Their Colors? Text copyright © 2006 by Jane Yolen.
Illustrations copyright © 2006 by Mark Teague.

How Do Dinosaurs Play with Their Friends? Text copyright © 2006 by Jane Yolen.
Illustrations copyright © 2006 by Mark Teague.

12 11 10 9 8 7 6 5 4 3 2   7 8 9 10 11 12/0

Printed in the U.S.A.   40

This edition first printing, September 2007

What if a dinosaur's
friends come to play?
Does he mope, does he pout
if he can't get his way?

STEGOSAURUS

Does he hide all his
dump trucks, refusing to share?

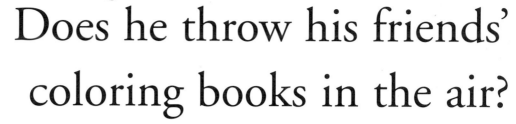

Does he throw his friends' coloring books in the air?

Does he hog all the swings and the sandbox and slides?

PROTOCERATOPS

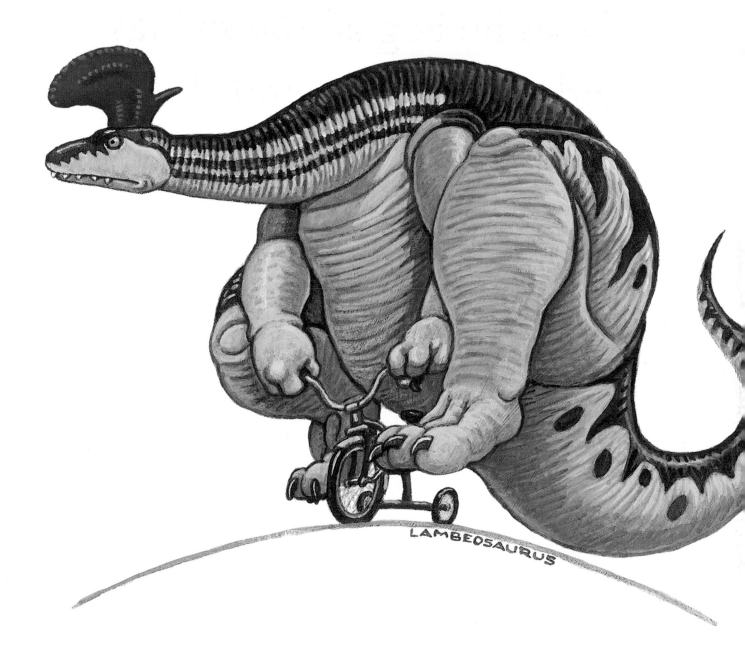

Does he not give his friends
any tricycle rides?

No, a dinosaur doesn't.
He knows how to play.
He treats everyone in the
friendliest way.

He shares all his toys,
and gives turns on his bike.

His friends get
first choice for the
games that they like.

He listens, then asks,
"Would you like
one turn more?"

Good friend,
good friend,
little
dinosaur.

Rainbows here,
and rainbows there. . . .

Dinosaur colors
everywhere!

and an **orange** backpack—
don't be late!

white chalk marks
on an old **black** slate,

brown circles
all around a date,

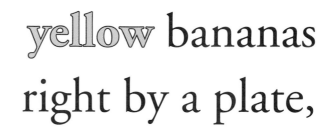

yellow bananas
right by a plate,

a **pink** ball
bouncing down
the stairs,

ANKYLOSAURUS

a **blue** robe thrown
across two chairs,

a **green** sign taped
to the bedroom door,

a **purple** towel
left on the floor,

GALLIMIMUS

GORGOSAURUS

A **red** fire truck
tucked under the bed,

Dinosaur colors
start with red:

How Do Dinosaurs Learn Their Colors?

SCHOLASTIC INC.
New York Toronto London Auckland Sydney
Mexico City New Delhi Hong Kong Buenos Aires

These books were originally published in hardcover by the Blue Sky Press in 2006.

ISBN-13: 978-0-545-01979-8
ISBN-10: 0-545-01979-6

12 11 10 9 8 7 6 5 4 3 2   7 8 9 10 11 12/0

Printed in the U.S.A.   40

This edition first printing, September 2007